JACK RUSSELL: Dog Detective

The Mugged Pug

DARREL & SALLY ODGERS

SCHOLASTIC CANADA LTD.

New York   Toronto   London   Auckland   Sydney
Mexico City   New Delhi   Hong Kong   Buenos Aires

Scholastic Canada Ltd.
604 King Street West, Toronto, Ontario M5V 1E1, Canada

Scholastic Inc.
557 Broadway, New York, NY 10012, USA

Scholastic Australia Pty Limited
PO Box 579, Gosford, NSW 2250, Australia

Scholastic New Zealand Limited
Private Bag 94407, Greenmount, Auckland, New Zealand

Scholastic Children's Books
Euston House, 24 Eversholt Street, London NW1 1DB, UK

Library and Archives Canada Cataloguing in Publication
Odgers, Darrel
The mugged pug / Darrel & Sally Odgers ; Janine Dawson, illustrator.

(Jack Russell, dog detective ; 3)
ISBN-13: 978-0-439-93800-6
ISBN-10: 0-439-93800-7

1. Dogs–Juvenile fiction. I. Odgers, Sally, 1957- II. Dawson, Janine
III. Title. IV. Series: Odgers, Darrel. Jack Russell, dog detective ; 3.
PZ7.O2374Mu 2007   j823'.92   C2006-905222-0

First published by Scholastic Press in 2005
Text copyright © by Sally and Darrel Odgers, 2005
Cover design copyright © Lake Shore Graphics, 2005
Cover photographs by Michael Bagnall
Dog, Sam, courtesy of Glenda Gould
Interior illustrations by Janine Dawson
Interior illustrations copyright © Scholastic Australia, 2005
All rights reserved.

6 5 4 3 2 1   Printed in Canada   06 07 08 09 10

Dear Readers,

The story you're about to
read is about me and my
friends, and how we solved the case of
the Mugged Pug. To save time, I'll
introduce us all to you now. Of course,
if you know us already, you can trot off
to Chapter One.

I am Jack Russell, Dog Detective.
I live with my landlord, Sarge, in
Doggeroo. Sarge detects human-type
crimes. I detect the crimes that deal
with dogs. I'm a Jack Russell terrier, so
I am dogged and intelligent.

Next door to Sarge and me live
Auntie Tidge and Foxy. Auntie Tidge is
lovely. She has biscuits. Foxy is not
lovely. He's a fox terrier (more or less).

He used to be a street dog, and a thief, but he's reformed now. Auntie Tidge has even gotten rid of his fleas. Foxy sometimes helps me with my cases.

Uptown Lord Setter (Lord Red for short) lives in Uptown House with Caterina Smith. Lord Red means well, but he isn't very bright.

We have other friends and acquaintances in Doggeroo. These include Polly the dachshund, Jill Russell, the squekes, Fat Molly Cat, and Shuffle the pug.

That's all you need to know, so let's get on with Chapter One.

Yours doggedly,

Jack Russell—the detective with a nose for crime

terrier-phone

Sarge and I were about to go out for our Saturday walk when the **terrier-phone** rang.

"I'd better get that, Jack," said Sarge. "It might be important."

I disagreed. Nothing is more important than Saturday walks, except food.

I **Jack-attacked** Sarge's pant leg to remind him, but Sarge went back into the house.

Since I was hanging on to his pants by my teeth, I went, too.

Sarge picked up the terrier-phone.

I stopped Jack-attacking his pants
long enough to find out who was
calling.

It was Ranger Jack.

Don't ask me why Doggeroo Dog
Control Officer Johnny Wolf calls
himself *Ranger Jack*. He just does.

"Straying dogs aren't police business, Ranger Jack," said Sarge to the terrier-phone. "It sounds like Walter Barkly's business to me."

Not police business? Then Sarge and I could go out for our walk. I trotted to the door.

"Can't you keep him at the pound until Walter comes back?" said Sarge. "Oh."

I yapped to remind Sarge that we had important things to do.

"I'll come now," said Sarge.

About time, too!

Sarge unhooked my leash, then he bent and undid my collar. "Sorry, Jack, I need this collar for someone else. You'll have to stay at home."

I didn't believe it. Sarge was giving away my *collar*? How could he?

Jack's Facts

My collar is old and comfortable.
It has my name on it. It smells like me.
My collar is perfect. It is **mine**.
This is a fact.

I Jack-attacked Sarge's pant leg again, but he just shook his head.

"Sorry, Jack," he said.

Sorry? He was taking away my own special collar and he was *sorry?*

After Sarge left, I went to visit Foxy and Auntie Tidge. Auntie Tidge was making **special biscuits**. Foxy was watching, scratching his ribs, and drooling.

"How's Jackie Wackie today?" Auntie Tidge is the only person who calls me that.

I whined, to show her how **pawly** I'd been treated. She bent down to pick me up. I gave her a slurp up her cheek that knocked her glasses sideways. She loves it when I do that.

"What are you after, Jack?" snarled Foxy. "This is *my* **terrier-tory**."

I ignored that. Foxy wouldn't even have a terrier-tory if I hadn't arranged for him to live with Auntie Tidge. He wouldn't have a new red collar, either.

"Where's your collar?" said Foxy, still scratching. "Sarge will be **pawfully** upset if you've lost it."

"He's putting it on someone else," I growled.

"Why?" said Foxy.

"How should I know?"

Foxy attacked the base of his tail

with his teeth. He doesn't have fleas now, but he has a **terrier-able** time getting rid of the old habit. "Thought you called yourself a detective," said Foxy through a mouthful of imaginary fleas.

I bristled. "I don't *call* myself a detective," I said. "I *am* a detective."

Jack's Glossary

Terrier-phones. *Things that ring.*

Jack-attack. *Growling and biting and tugging at pant legs. Very loud. Quite harmless.*

Special biscuits. *Auntie Tidge makes these. They don't harm terrier teeth.*

Pawly. *Poorly, badly.*

Terrier-tory. *Territory owned by a terrier.*

Pawfully. *Very.*

Terrier-able. *Same as terrible, but to do with terriers.*

In-terrier-gation

Sarge had taken the car to wherever he had gone. I'm the best tracking Jack in the business, but I knew I wouldn't be **pupular** if I went out without my collar.

Jack's Facts

Special dogs need special people.
A special collar says a dog has a special person.
Dogs without special people can end up in the pound.
This is a fact.

"*You* go," I said to Foxy. "You're my second-in-command."

"Go where?" Foxy was still working on that itch.

"Follow Sarge," I said.

Foxy scratched his ear. "Send Red," he said.

I started giving Foxy all the reasons why I couldn't send Red to spy on Sarge. I still hadn't finished when we heard Sarge come back.

I jumped up. By the time Sarge reached the gate, I was lying in my basket with my nose on my paws. I sighed, loudly.

Jack's Facts

When you have been badly treated, you have to show it.
If you don't show the way you feel, no one will be sorry for you.
This is a fact.

"Cheer up, Jack," said Sarge. "I've brought you a visitor." Shuffle the pug followed Sarge. He was wheezing loudly. He was wearing *my* collar. The one I had had for three years. The one with my name on it.

"What are you doing here?" I yapped. "You belong down near the reserve with Walter Barkly."

Shuffle snuffled, then plunked down with his jaw on his paws.

<u>Jack's Facts</u>

Most dogs lie with their noses on their
paws.
Pugs have their noses in a different place.
Therefore, pugs lie with their jaws on
their paws.
This is a fact.

"Well?" I said. No Jack wants a pug moving into his terrier-tory without **pawmission**. Especially when the pug is wearing the Jack's collar. I had a bad feeling about this. Shuffle knew he should have asked pawmission to enter my terrier-tory. He hadn't. So something was very wrong.

Shuffle sighed. "I've had a horrible day."

So had I, but at least now I was interviewing a witness. Or a suspect. Or maybe both. I began my **in-terrier-gation**.

"Why are you wearing my collar?"

"Ranger Jack caught me without my collar," snuffled Shuffle. "He took me to the pound. It was horrible, Jack!"

I thought about Shuffle's collar. It is

a new bright blue one, with a silver pug ornament. *I* wouldn't wear it, but Shuffle thinks it's **pawfect**.

"Why didn't Walter Barkly come and get you?" I asked.

"Walter Barkly is away for the weekend." Shuffle put his paws over his eyes.

"Pull yourself together, pug," I barked. "Where did Ranger Jack catch you?"

"I was coming home from Uptown House," muttered Shuffle. "Walter Barkly left me with Caterina Smith. Lord Red kept bothering me, so I started walking home to wait for Walter Barkly."

"So," I said, "Ranger Jack caught you without your collar. Walter Barkly wasn't home, so he called Sarge on the terrierphone to come and get you."

"That's right," snuffled Shuffle. "The pound is full. The pug-mugger's taken so many collars that there are a lot of dogs waiting for their owners."

"Pug-mugger? What's a pug-mugger?"

"Pug-muggers mug pugs and other dogs and steal their collars," said Shuffle.

"Hmm," I said. I hadn't known this, but I wasn't going to admit this fact to Shuffle.

I decided right then that I'd take the case.

Jack's Glossary

Pupular. *Popular, only used for dogs.*

Pawmission. *Permission, only for dogs.*

In-terrier-gation. *Same as interrogation, but done by a terrier.*

Pawfect. *Perfect, only used for dogs.*

A Mugged Pug or a Mug of a Pug?

Shuffle said he'd been pug-mugged just before Ranger Jack arrived.

"Sure you didn't just lose your collar?" I asked. "Maybe you caught it on a branch when you were leaving Uptown House."

"Maybe a Jack Russell doesn't know a branch from a pug-mugger. But any pug will tell you—"

"That's enough!" I **Jack-yapped**.

That brought Sarge out. I didn't Jack-attack his leg this time. I turned my back and sniffed, to let him know he was still in the **doghouse**.

That's when I smelled something interesting.

I did a quick **nose map**.

Jack's Map

1. Beef cooking in the kitchen.

2. My blanket that Auntie Tidge knit for me.

3. Foxy.

4. Auntie Tidge baking special biscuits.

5. Sarge's coffee steaming.

Hmm, it wasn't any of those.

"What's all the noise about, Jack?" asked Sarge.

Sniff-sniff. I focused my **super-sniffer** on Shuffle.

6. My collar.

7. Shuffle.

Hmm. I sniff-sniffed again. A plan was forming in my mind, but I needed my collar to carry it out. **Flea soap**! I needed my collar in any case.

I didn't want to forgive Sarge yet, but Jack Russell, Dog Detective, isn't a dog to let a grudge stand in the way of a good lead, so I did the **paw thing** to show Sarge what I wanted.

Sarge laughed. "Oh, all right, Jack." He unbuckled my collar from Shuffle's neck. "I guess you won't be needing a collar in our yard, boy," he said to Shuffle. "And from what Ranger Jack says, you're not the only dog without a collar in Doggeroo."

He buckled the collar on me, and I gave him a quick Jack-attack as a reward. I had my collar—my pawfect comfy collar. I also had backup for Shuffle's statement that dogs were losing collars. "Stay here," I said to Shuffle.

"Where are you going, Jack?"

"To interview a witness," I said. "Either you really have been **collared**, mugged, and de-collared, or else you're just a mug of a pug."

<u>Jack's Facts</u>

Fences are to keep other dogs out, not to keep Jacks in.
Jacks jump over.

Jacks burrow under.
Jacks squirm through.
This is a fact.

I left the yard (never mind how) and headed for Uptown House. On the way, I saw three squekes doing what squekes do in Dora Barkins's yard.

"Are you wearing collars?" I asked sternly.

"What's it to you, Jack?" yipped the squekes.

"Answer in the name of the paw!" I said. "Are you wearing your collars?"

The squekes flew at the gate, yipping. Their hair blew back in the wind and I saw their old brown collars. A formal interview was not necessary. I had to see Lord Red.

Jack's Glossary

Jack-yap. *Shrill, very loud yap, yapped by a Jack.*

Doghouse. *For a person to be in a doghouse is a disgrace. For a dog, it's pawfectly fine.*

Nose map. *Way of storing information collected by the nose.*

Super-sniffer. *Jack's nose in super-tracking mode.*

Flea soap. *A terrier-able swear word.*

Paw thing. *Up on hind legs, paws held together as if praying. Means pleased excitement.*

Collared. *Grabbed by the collar.*

Red at the Ready

When I reached Uptown House, Lord
Red was rushing about, whirling his tail.

"Shuffle, come out now! Shuffle,
Shuffle, where are you?" he barked.

"Red, get your paws over here!" I
yapped.

"Jack, Jack, is that you Jack? Jack,
Jack, come and help me find Shuffle.
We are playing hide—"

"Stop that, Red!" I growled.
"Shuffle isn't here."

"Yes, he is. We're playing hide-and-
squeak. Shuffle, Shuffle! Where are you?"

"Halt!" I barked.

Red skidded to a halt. "Yes, Jack? Have you come to play, Jack?"

"I'm on a case," I said.

"Can I help, Jack, please?"

"Settle down," I commanded. "Sit. Stay. Drop."

Red sat, stayed, and dropped.

I in-terrier-gated Red, and this is what I learned.

1. Shuffle the pug *had* been staying with Caterina Smith and Red while Walter Barkly was away.
2. Shuffle *had* been wearing a collar when Red last saw him.
3. It was a nice, new, blue leather collar with a silver pug emblem.
4. Red had no idea when Shuffle had left Uptown House.

"He was here just now," said Red. "Has Shuffle disappeared, Jack? Has he been **dognapped**? What can I do?"

I told Red to stand by. "And *don't* lose your collar," I said.

"Never!" said Red. "It's brand-new. Besides, Caterina Smith says dogs without collars go to the poooound!"

The pug really had been mugged. Now I had to find the person who had done it.

I trotted home past the flea market. As I crossed the overpass, I met a person eating a pie. He snapped his fingers at me.

Jack's Facts

It pays to approach people eating pies.
People eating pies drop crumbs.
Some dogs say pies might be poison.
People don't eat poisoned pies.
This is *a fact*.

The pie-person gave me a bite of pie, rubbed my neck, and told me to run home.

Jack's Glossary

Dognapped. Kidnapped, only done to a dog.

Flea market. A market for humans and dogs, not fleas.

Orange Odor

When I got home, Shuffle was sulking on our porch. There were two big beef bones in front of him. I picked one up. A **Jack-snack** is always welcome.

Shuffle sighed.

"Aren't you hungry?" I began to gnaw my bone.

"I'm too sad." Shuffle put his jaw back on his paws.

"Foxy will guzzle it if you don't watch out," I warned.

"Who cares?" said Shuffle. "What will Walter Barkly say when he finds out I've been mugged?"

"He won't know," I said. "He'll think you lost your collar."

I picked up the other bone and carried it to the corner of the yard. Then I dug a hole and buried it.

Shuffle whined.

"Cheer up," I said. "Jack Russell's the name, detection's the game. I'll get your collar back."

"How?" said Shuffle.

Jack's Facts

Jacks can do anything.
They don't always know exactly how they're going to do it.
That doesn't mean it won't be done.
This is a fact.

"I need to discuss the case with my second-in-command."

I barked for Foxy to come over.

We waited. No Foxy.

"Foxy!" I barked. "Get your paws over here!"

We waited. No Foxy.

"Looks like your second-in-command's ignoring you," said Shuffle.

"He must be out with Auntie Tidge," I corrected.

I did a quick nose map.

Jack's Map

1. Beef cooling in the kitchen.

2. Fading smell of Auntie
   Tidge's special biscuits.

3. A whiff of buried beef bone.

4. Fat Molly Cat from the library
   trotting up the street.

5. Foxy in Auntie Tidge's yard.

What???

Foxy was just on the other side of the hedge? Ignoring me?

"Foxy, get yourself here, pronto!" I Jack-yapped.

We waited. No Foxy.

I trotted over to the hedge. Foxy was definitely there. I could smell him. I sniff-sniffed, and smelled something else. An **orange odor**.

I **Jack-jumped** so I could see over the hedge.

There was Foxy, hiding under a bush.

"Foxy," I growled. "Get over here."

Foxy crept toward the gap between his
terrier-tory and mine.

"What's wrong with him?" asked
Shuffle. "Has someone mugged him and
stolen his new collar?"

Foxy crawled up to the porch and then
rolled over. "*This* is what's wrong,"
he growled. "Look!"

We looked.

Foxy's belly was bright orange.

Jack's Glossary

Jack-snack. *A snack for a Jack.*

Orange odor. *A smell that is bright orange.*

Jack-jump. *A sudden spring made by a Jack.*

Super-Sniffer

No Jack laughs when a pal's been painted orange. It was just coincidence that I had to go and have a long **Jack-lap** from my water bowl.

While I was Jack-lapping, Shuffle asked, "What's that?"

Foxy was too ashamed to speak, so I answered for him.

"It's Auntie Tidge's anti-itch lotion," I said. "Foxy was scratching too much."

"So?" grumbled Foxy. "What's so terrier-able about that? I *like* to scratch."

Jack's Facts

Dogs like to scratch.
Humans don't like dogs to scratch.
Too much scratching leads to flea baths
or to being painted orange.
This is a fact.

I told Foxy to scratch in private. Just then Red came tearing down the street.

"Jack, Jack! Jaaaack!"

Foxy, Shuffle, and I scooted down the porch steps. Red sailed over the fence and landed right on top of my **squeaker-bone.**

"Sorrrry!" yelped Red, and sailed back over the fence.

A few seconds later, he stuck his long nose back into my terrier-tory. "Did

I squash you, Jack? Did I?"

"Do I *look* squashed?"

"You squeaked," said Red.

"My squeaker-bone squeaked," I corrected. "You might as well come in."

Red sailed over the fence for a third time. He stared at Shuffle. "Why are you here, Shuffle? I thought we were playing hide-and-squeak?" Then he stared at Foxy. "Why is your belly orange, Foxy? Is

Jack investigating your case?"

"Foxy's orange belly has no bearing on the case, Red," I said.

Well, that's what I thought at the time.

"Won't Caterina Smith be looking for you?" I added.

"Caterina Smith is looking for Shuffle down at the reserve," said Red. "I got lonely after Caterina Smith left. That's why I came to see you, Jack. And do you know what, Jack? I nearly lost my new collar on the way!"

"How could you *nearly* lose your collar?" asked Shuffle.

"I was running past the flea market when a kind man stopped me. He said my collar was loose. It's new, and the silver thing hadn't gone into the leather thing properly. He fixed it for me." Red's eyes gleamed. "Wasn't that kind of him? He said I was a good doggie!"

I Jack-jumped up to check his new collar.

"It's not loose now, Jack," said Red.

"No," I said. "It isn't even there! Your *kind man* was really the pug-mugger!"

"But he *helped* me with my lovely new collar, Jack!" Red said.

"He was *mugging* you," I said. "You *know* not to play with strangers!"

"Of course," said Red. "Caterina Smith says I might get dognapped. But he wasn't a dognapper."

"He mugged you and stole your collar," said Shuffle.

"He *fixed* my collar," insisted Red. "The silver thing didn't fit in the leather thing because it's so new! Why would he steal my collar? I'm worth a fistful of dollars. Who would steal my collar and not dognap *me*?"

This case was getting complicated.

I Jack-yapped for order. "We have a suspect now," I said, "and two witnesses."

"Who, Jack? Are you going to in-terrier-gate them, Jack? Can I help, Jack?"

"Not unless you want to in-terrier-gate yourself, Red," I said. "You're one witness. Shuffle is the other."

"I'm a victim, not a witness!" snapped Shuffle. "I'm a mugged pug!"

"A victim can also be a witness," I explained. (I've heard Sarge say that.) "You must think back."

"Are you going to **yip-notize** us, Jack?" asked Red. "Are you?"

"No," I said. "Tell me everything you

remember about the pug-mugger."

Shuffle said the pug-mugger was big.
Red said he wasn't. Shuffle said he'd
growled at the mugger. Red said he hadn't.

"Maybe he was nice to you because
you've got big teeth," I said to Red.
"Unless there are *two* muggers."

I used my super-sniffer. First, I sniff-
sniffed Shuffle. The smell of the pug-
mugger was fading, because Shuffle had
been with Ranger Jack and with Sarge.

But there was still a faint trace. I
sniff-sniffed to fix it in my **smellbank**.

Then I checked Red for the same
trace. Red squirmed and complained
I was messing up his ears. Foxy
threatened to swing off them instead.

"You'll make me all orange!"
protested Red.

"The orange only comes off when it's wet," snarled Foxy. "Otherwise, you'd be wearing it already."

While Foxy was explaining the orange odor, I finished sniff-sniffing Red. Success! "I can dogmatically state," I announced, "that the pug-mugger who attacked Shuffle is the *same* mugger who stole Red's collar."

I waited for **appaws**, but the others were staring—Shuffle and Foxy through the gate and Red over the gate.

Their ears (and mine) had picked up a familiar cry.

"Lordie, *Lordie*! Lordieeeeee!"

"Here comes Caterina Smith," said Red. He sailed over the gate for a fourth time, and **greeted** Caterina Smith. Then he sailed over the gate for the fifth time.

He landed on my squeaker-bone, again.

Caterina Smith dashed through the gate. "Lordie, you naughty, *naughty* boy! Shuffle, what are you doing here? I've been looking everywhere for you!"

Sarge came out to see what was going on. Sarge might not be the brightest biscuit in the box, but he knows trouble when he smells it.

"Calm down, Caterina," he said. "What's going on?"

"Why didn't you call and tell me Lordie and Shuffle were here?" snapped Caterina Smith. "Walter Barkly left him with me and he disappeared! I went pug-hunting and then Lordie disappeared. Now they've lost their collars!"

"I didn't know Shuffle was supposed

to be at your house," said Sarge. "As for Lordie, he just arrived. Now you can take them both home. We could put Jack's collar back on Shuffle, and maybe Foxy's will . . ."

I didn't wait for Sarge to finish, and neither did Foxy. Both of us shot out of the yard (never mind how) and went to hide under Auntie Tidge's bed.

Jack's Glossary

Jack-lap. *A drink lapped out of a water bowl by a Jack.*

Squeaker-bone. *Item for exercising a Jack's jaws. Not to be confused with a toy.*

Jack's Glossary

Yip-notize. To *hypnotize, as practiced by a terrier.*

Smellbank. *A dog's collection of remembered smells.*

Appaws. *Cheering and paw-prancing to praise a clever act.*

Greeted. *This is done by rising on the hind legs and clutching a person with the paws while slurping their face.*

Jack on the Track

Sarge drove Caterina Smith, Lord Red, and Shuffle back to Uptown House.

As soon as they left, Foxy and I crawled out from under Auntie Tidge's bed.

"If we're quick, we might be able to track the pug-mugger," I said.

I sniffed the air a few times to clear my smellbank, and then put my super-sniffer to work on a quick nose map.

Jack's Map

1. Fat Molly sunning herself on a wall.

2. The three squekes playing with a dehydrated rat.

3. Dora Barkins's sheepskin coat.

4. The buried beef bone.

5. Sarge's cold coffee.

6. A whiff of biscuit
from Auntie Tidge.

7. The orange odor on Foxy.

8. Six sparrows squabbling
under a bush.

9. Red's pawprints.

Some dogs might have wasted time tracking Fat Molly or the rat, or **terrier-izing** the sparrows, but not a tracking Jack. My super-sniffer fixed on the right scent and I began to track.

With Foxy trotting after me, I tracked my way past the three squekes, and turned right toward the flea market.

Sniff-sniff, sniff-sniff, I followed Red's original trail. The closer we got to the flea market, the stronger the trace of the pug-mugger became.

When we were near the overpass, even Foxy could smell it.

"He went *this* way," I said.

Sniff-sniff, sniff-sniff. Red-scent, pug-mugger-scent.

"Hey, Jack!" yapped Foxy. "Wait!"

Sniff-sniff, sniff-sniff. Red-scent, pug-mugger-scent, pie-person-scent. I tracked on.

Jack's Facts

A tracking Jack never leaves the trail.
A tracking Jack takes no notice of
*anything **but** the trail.*
This is mostly a fact.

The pie-person-scent got stronger. This was a problem. A really strong pie-smell can distract even a tracking Jack. Suddenly, pie-person was all I could smell. He was on the overpass, eating another pie.

I stopped, and sniff-sniffed. Foxy was drooling.

"You again, Jack?" said the pie-person. "Off you go."

Some people understand about tracking Jacks. The pie-person could see I was busy with a case. As I sniff-sniffed on, I heard guzzling behind me.

Foxy was feasting.

Foxy used to be a street dog. He *never* passes up a snack.

I tracked on.

When I reached the flea market, the pug-mugger-scent had faded.

"That's odd," I said.

"What's odd?" Foxy trotted up beside me, licking his chops.

"The mugger—" I stared at Foxy. "Foxy, where's your collar?"

"My *collar?*" Foxy scratched at his neck with his claw. "It's fallen off."

"**Dogwash!**" I said. "It was a new one. It was bright red and shiny."

Foxy turned three times, trying to see his neck. Then he gave up and sat down.

Quickly, I nose-mapped Foxy.

1. Foxy.
2. Orange odor.
3. Pie.
4. Auntie Tidge.
5. Special biscuits.
6. The mugger.

Foxy had definitely been in contact with the mugger, but where? When?

"I've got it!" I yapped. "I've cracked the case!"

I waited for appaws, but Foxy just looked **foxed**.

"The pie-person!" I explained. "The pie-person is the mugger. Don't you see, Foxy? He stole your collar while you were guzzling pie!"

"Dogwash," said Foxy. "Red and Shuffle never mentioned pies."

"He uses different methods for different victims," I said. "Shuffle's easy to grab, so the mugger grabbed him. Red is easy to trick, so the mugger pretended to help him. You're easy to bribe, so he bribed you with pie."

"What about *you*, Jack?' snarled Foxy.

"He could see there's no point bribing me," I said.

"Or maybe you're just not worth mugging?" Foxy sneered.

"We both met the pie-person-pug-mugger," I said, "and which of us still has his collar?"

I knew we were on the right track now. We had a suspect. We knew he could have mugged the dogs of Doggeroo. What we didn't know was *why*. To find out, we raced back to the overpass, but the suspect had gone.

"He's not getting away with this," I stated.

We picked up his scent and tracked the suspect to the library. Fat Molly was washing herself on the step. She called us something rude in **catspeak**, but we took no notice. We tracked to the police station. Then we tracked up the hill to the other entrance to the flea market.

People were already setting up stalls

for the next day.

That's where we sniffed down the suspect. We hid behind a hot dog stand and watched him unload things from a van.

I wanted to terrier-ize him into giving us back the collars, but terrier-izing people gets terriers into trouble. Besides—it isn't as easy as you might think.

Jack's Facts

Jacks are brave.

Jacks are bold.

Jacks are not the biggest dogs in the world.

Some people don't take them seriously.

This is a fact.

"Will Sarge arrest him?" asked Foxy.

"Maybe, but first we need to set up a **doggo obbo**," I decided. "We need to find out where the suspect is hiding the collars. We also need to figure out his motive."

"Maybe he has a lot of dogs?" suggested Foxy. "Why else would he steal Red's and my collars, but not Red and me?"

I looked at him. "What dognapper would want you, Foxy?"

"Or you?" snapped Foxy. "This one didn't even want your silly old collar!"

My hackles rose, but now wasn't the time to fight with Foxy. We had some **skulldoggery** to stop.

Our doggo obbo didn't last long. Ranger Jack came in one showground gate, so we slipped out the other. We couldn't risk him catching Foxy without his collar. Besides, it was dinnertime.

<u>Jack's Facts</u>

Doggo obbos are important.
So is avoiding Ranger Jack.
Dinner is the most important thing of all.
This is a fact.

Jack's Glossary

Terrier-izing. *Frightening.*

Dogwash. *Nonsense.*

Foxed. *Puzzled, as only a fox terrier can be.*

Catspeak. *The way cats talk.*

Doggo obbo. *An observation carried out by dogs.*

Skulldoggery. *Something bad concerning dogs.*

Steak-Out

Auntie Tidge was angry that Foxy
had lost his collar. So Foxy had to be
fast on his feet to join me at the
doggo obbo the next morning. We
arranged a **steak-out** behind the hot
dog stand.

At first, everything was quiet.
Then the suspect came out of the van
and began to set up his stall. He laid
out watches, pens, and other small
things. Then he laid out some dog
collars. They all had blue tags.

We were about to fetch Sarge to
make an arrest, when Caterina Smith

walked past the hot dog van. She approached the suspect.

"Bother!" I said. "She'll find Red's collar. Then she'll get the credit for solving *my* case!"

Caterina Smith picked up some collars. She shook her head and put them down again. The suspect fetched another bunch of collars from the van. These had yellow tags.

Caterina Smith took one. She smiled. She gave the suspect some money and went back up the hill to Uptown House.

"What's going on?" I asked. "Why didn't she recognize Red's collar?"

Foxy scratched his belly even though Auntie Tidge had re-oranged him. "Would *you* recognize Red's collar?"

"Of course," I said. "It smells like Red."

Gloria Smote came by, carrying Polly the dachshund. Polly snarled at the suspect, and struggled to get down.

"Naughty!" said Gloria Smote. "You can't get down without your collar. You know what Ranger Jack said."

She bought a collar from the suspect.

"That's not Polly's collar," I said.

Gloria Smote put the collar on Polly, and carried her away.

During the first hour of our steak-out, we saw Jill Russell, and three other dogs I didn't know. All their people bought collars from the suspect.

Could I be barking up the wrong tree? Could the suspect be innocent?

No. There was evidence against him. He *must* have stolen Foxy's collar.

I left the steak-out and trotted over to the suspect's stall. I sniff-sniffed about. I was *sure* I could smell Foxy's collar. And Red's. And Polly's collar, too.

I Jack-jumped so I could see the collars on the stall.

"You again, Jack!" said the suspect. "What do you want?"

"He's shopping for a new collar," said the hot dog man.

I Jack-jumped again, and sniff-sniffed. I could still smell Foxy's collar, but I couldn't see it.

I went back to Foxy. "I can tell you one thing," I said. "These collars aren't brand new."

"Where's my collar?" asked Foxy.

"I think the Doggeroo collars are stashed in the van. Which means . . . well, you know what *that* means, Foxy!"

It meant I had all the facts I needed to make an arrest. We knew the guilty person.

We knew he had used force, trickery, and bribery.

"And we even know *why* he did it," I told Foxy.

"Do we?" said Foxy.

I sighed.

Sometimes, Foxy just isn't entirely **on the ball**!

Jack's Glossary

Steak-out. *A place where detectives can watch suspects and eat at the same time.*

On the ball. *Dogs chase balls. Clever dogs always jump on them to stop them from rolling.*

Jack-pack Attack

"The suspect has been clever," I said. "If he hadn't come to Doggeroo, he might have kept on mugging pugs (and bribing fox terriers and fooling setters) forever.

"Here's what I think he's been doing. One: the pug-mugger goes to Town One and steals collars; two: he moves to Town Two and steals more collars; three: in Town Two, he sells the collars from Town One to the people whose dogs he mugged in Town Two; four: he moves to Town Three and steals more collars; five: he sells the collars from Town Two to the people whose dogs he mugged in Town Three; and so on."

I sat back and waited for appaws.

Instead, Foxy scratched his ribs. "So that's why he didn't mug *you*, Jack. Nobody would want your *old* collar."

"*I* want my collar!" I snapped. "It's special. Sarge gave it to me."

"And I want mine!" snarled Foxy. "Mine is special. Auntie Tidge gave it to me."

I sighed. I'd solved the case, but that didn't get the collars back.

"I think this calls for backup from the **Jack-pack**," I said.

"Run around the market and alert all the dogs you can find," I told Foxy. "I'll get Red and Shuffle and the squekes. We need lots of fuss and yips. *Nobody* can yip like the squekes."

Foxy trotted off, and I ran to Uptown House. Red was playing hide-and-squeak by himself. Shuffle was snuffling under a bush.

"Jack, Jack, I've got another collar!" barked Red. "And Jack, do you know what, Jack? My new collar smells just like the kind man who took my other collar. Isn't that funny, Jack?"

Jack's Facts

Most dogs are brighter than you think. A few of them are dimmer than you would believe. This is a fact.

"Not very," I said. "He stole your collar to sell. Then he sold Caterina Smith one that belonged to someone else. He's still got yours. And we have to find it."

"Can I help you find it, Jack? Can I?"

"What about mine?" asked Shuffle.

"He's still got yours, too," I said. "Come on! We're going to get them back!"

Red sailed over the fence. Shuffle crammed himself through a gap. (Never mind how it got there.) I sent Shuffle straight to the flea market. Red and I dashed around Doggeroo calling for backup.

Did it work? Of course it did! No Doggeroo dog would miss the chance to run with the Jack-pack! In half an hour, the Jack-pack was trotting toward the flea market. Three minutes after that, fifty-nine dogs dashed through the market and gathered at the hot dog stand. We were almost ready to storm the suspect's stall.

"What are we waiting for?" yipped the squekes.

"Wait!" I Jack-yapped.

I cocked my ears. Any minute now . . .

"Lordie, *Lordie*! Lordieeeeee!"

"Polly, you come back here!"

"Jill, Jill! Oh, you *naughty* dog!"

"Lordie, *Lordie*! Lordieeeeee!"

"Foxy Woxy, Jackie Wackie!"

"Jack? Where are you?"

"That's what we're waiting for!" I said.

Our people came rushing (and puffing) toward the hot dog stand. Caterina Smith was in the lead, followed by Gloria Smote, and Dora Barkins. Sarge was making pretty good speed. Panting along behind him was Auntie Tidge.

At the back came Ranger Jack.

"Jack-pack! ATTACK!" I ordered. We launched ourselves at the suspect's stall.

Jack's Glossary

Jack-pack. *A noble pack of dogs united under a strong leader.*

The Orange-odor Plan

We didn't hurt the suspect. Jack-pack
attacks are all about noise and
attracting backup. Some of us ran
around and around the stall. This
stopped the suspect from escaping.
Some of us gathered around the van.
This showed the backup people where
to look.

I sniff-sniffed to make sure the
goods were still inside.

They were.

The squekes yipped. Red sailed
over the stall. Jill and Polly and
Shuffle milled around. It was a sea of

dogs, a posse of pups! It was all part of the plan.

Foxy sneaked into the hot dog stand and ate three hot dogs.

That *wasn't* part of the plan.

"Jack, what *is* this?" Sarge sounded a bit annoyed.

This was my big moment. I sniffed loudly at the van, and then did the paw thing.

Sarge looked sternly at the suspect. "I'm Sergeant Russell," he said, "of the Doggeroo Police."

"Oh," said the suspect.

"Is this your van, sir?" asked Sarge. "Can you explain what my dog finds so interesting about it?"

The suspect looked at me. "You *again*, Jack?" He sighed. "What kind of

place has police dogs going undercover
as Jack Russell terriers?"

That was almost the end of the Case
of the Mugged Pug. The suspect gave
back the Doggeroo collars. Sarge took
the rest of the stock into custody.

It wasn't quite the end, though.
Catching a criminal is one thing.
Preventing crime is even more important.
I had a plan to make sure no one ever
stole another Doggeroo dog collar.

"How will we do that, Jack?" asked
Red.

"We'll mark the collars," I said.
"Foxy? Think you can steal the orange-
odor lotion from Auntie Tidge's
cupboard?"